Welcome to the Disney Learning Programme

Sharing a book with your children is the perfect opportunity to cuddle and enjoy the reading experience together. Research has shown that reading aloud to and with your children is one of the most important ways to prepare them for success as a reader.

When you share books with each other, you help strengthen your children's reading and vocabulary skills as well as stimulate their curiosity, imagination and enthusiasm for reading.

Cars 3 tells the story of hotshot racing car, Lightning McQueen. Used to being the best, McQueen's top spot is suddenly challenged by a new superstar car. He must work hard with the help of his friends if he is to become the Piston Cup champion once again.

You can help your children enjoy the story even more by talking to them about how family and friends help each other. Children find it easier to understand what they read when they can connect it with their own personal experiences.

Children learn in different ways and at different speeds, but they all require a supportive environment to nurture a lifelong love of books, reading and learning. The Adventures in Reading books are carefully levelled to present new challenges to developing readers. They are filled with familiar and fun characters from the wonderful world of Disney to make the learning experience comfortable, positive and enjoyable.

Enjoy your reading adventure together!

Scholastic Children's Books
Euston House,
24 Eversholt Street,
London NW1 1DB, UK

A division of Scholastic Ltd
London ~ New York ~ Toronto ~ Sydney ~ Auckland
Mexico City ~ New Delhi ~ Hong Kong

First published in the United States by Random House Children's Books in 2017
Published in the UK by Scholastic Ltd, 2017

ISBN 978 1407 16588 2

Printed in Slovakia by TBB

2 4 6 8 10 9 7 5 3 1

www.scholastic.co.uk

Back on Track!

by Susan Amerikaner
illustrated by the
Disney Storybook Art Team

Lightning McQueen
is one of the
greatest racers
of all time.

He is faster than fast.

He is speed!

Sterling owns the new
Rust-eze Racing Centre.

He is a big fan
of Lightning McQueen!

Cruz Ramirez
trains racing cars.
She dreams of
racing one day.

Lightning is out of shape.

Cruz trains him.

She wants to make him

a great racer again.

Mack is a big truck.

He drives Lightning

all over the country.

Luigi and Guido are part
of Lightning's pit crew.
Luigi chooses tyres.
Guido changes them.

Jackson Storm is

a new kind

of racing car.

He is young.

He is fast.

He keeps winning.

He even beats
Lightning!

Doc Hudson was
a great racer.
He taught Lightning
to love racing.

Lightning watches
old films
of Doc racing.
Lightning misses Doc.

Smokey was
Doc Hudson's crew chief.
Now he trains Lightning
for the next big race.

Lightning is not
as fast as he was.
He must race better.

Mr Drippy
waters the track
at Thunder Hollow.

Miss Fritter is queen
of the Thunder Hollow
Crazy Eight Derby.
She loves
to crash.

Darrell calls the action
at the Piston Cup.
Chick Hicks was a racer.
Now he has a TV show.

Natalie Certain is a guest
on Chick's show.
She says Jackson Storm
will win.

Louise Nash

was a racing star

long ago.

Now she gives Cruz

racing tips.

Cruz races.

Her dream comes true.

She is happy that

Lightning is her teammate!

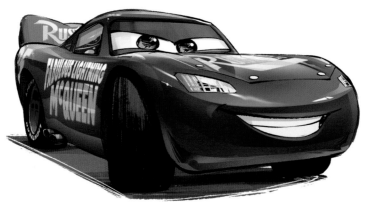